ZOIE

'I Don't think Jesus did it this way.'

by Jack Webb

Published by Theoria Publishing, 2024.

ZOIE 'I DON'T THINK JESUS DID IT THIS WAY.'

First edition. September 17, 2024.

Copyright © 2024 Jack Webb.

ISBN: 979-8990736917

Written by Jack Webb.

Table of Contents

For

Peri

When a man loves a woman
Can't keep his mind on nothing else
He'll trade the world for the good thing he's found
If she's bad he can't see it
She can do no wrong
Turns his back on his best friend
If he puts her down
– Percy Sledge

Lord Jesus Christ,
Son of God,
have mercy on me,
a sinner.
– The Jesus Prayer

1

MOMMA'S HOUSE—THURS.—1 AUG.—5:42 AM

LIKE A CAT PLAYING with a wounded mouse, a fierce thunderstorm is having its way with Willburn, Texas. As the lightning strobes in bright silence, relentless thunder shakes the buildings. The assault is fierce. The whole town is like a doomed passenger train rocketing into hell.

In the smallest room of the house, the only light is from the lightning strobing maniacally through the window in the shower. Chris—age 24—is getting up from his knees and pushing himself away from the toilet. His head is pounding like a jackhammer factory. Weak and trembling, he grabs the counter and lifts himself up to the sink. It should be safe now. His belly is empty. The endless dry heaves have proven that. Barely able to stand, he leans all his weight on the counter and lets his head sag toward the bowl. This position provides some relief from his pounding headache. Chris wipes his fouled lips with the back of a trembling hand. He wants to look the best he can before gazing into this morning's impeccable mirror.

It has been this way for a while now. Since he finished college and the economy crashed, the idleness, drinking and the drugs have taken him. Chris is a full-time party person now.

Grimacing with each strike of thunder, he lifts his head up and looks into the flashing mirror light. Chris is stunned to find a sweat soaked corpse looking back at him. "Lord, please help me. I can't take this anymore," he mutters as he lowers himself down to the cool tile floor and sleeps there for a while.

8:05 am...

Chris is at his mother's kitchen table, with an ice cold glass bottle of Mexican Coca-Cola in one hand and ten-buffered aspirin in the other.

His mother, Donka, plops a steaming bowl of oatmeal with cinnamon and sliced bananas in front of him. Chris quickly slides his chair back and looks at the bowl with deep suspicion. Satisfied it is only oatmeal, he fills his mouth with Coca-Cola, tilts his head back, throws in all ten aspirin, and swallows.

He carefully puts the empty bottle on the table and takes a deep breath. Then he looks pitifully at his mother through watery bloodshot eyes.

Donka is leaning against the sink with her arms crossed, looking at her son. She has a large-round head that reminds Chris of a jack-o'-lantern.

"Drunk again," she explodes in her thick Bulgarian accent.

Chris winces in pain from the high-volume delivery of her words.

She continues anyway. "You were doing so good, Chris. You were going to your meetings and now? Here you are drunk, again!" Donka breaks down and sobs into her towel before throwing it into the dishwater. A flood of tears, black with mascara, flow down her cheeks as she glares at him with fire in her eyes.

"Yes, Mother." Chris responds, struggling to hold the aspirin down and not just puke on the floor.

"Don't you 'Yes mother' me! You a smarts-a-ass!" She screams.

Chris hangs on to the seat bottom and resists covering his ears while she continues. "We give you an American name and an honorable skill from the old country, and all you do with it is get drunk and make sex with whores."

"Ok Momma, I…" Chris says, moving to hold his pounding head with both hands before she interrupts, "You go to a meeting today or else, buddy."

"Ok Momma. I will, I promise."

"I'm just not happy, Momma." Chris pleads, then surprises himself with an outrageous burp. "Oh, my god!" He apologizes. "I'm so sorry Momma. My life is just a mess. I'm a comedian. I just want to make people laugh. See.."

"See? I see!" She shouts. "Do you see how sorry those comedians on TV are, huh?"

"Yes, Momma, you've told me," Chris says, struggling to sit up straighter.

"They all look like frightened marsupeeze."

"Marsupials. I think you mean marsupials Momma. Please don't shout." Chris begs.

"Oh well, alright, but you know what? They take drugs all the time just so they can talk. Then they never shuts up."

"You are thinking of Billy Bunns from Canada, Momma. He is a very successful Momma."

"He looks like a starved, marsupee! How's a man that talks like that—that dirty talk he talk—ever going to get a decent woman?"

"Momma, he has tons of women!" Chris realizes his error and tenses for the hurricane to come.

"Whores! Whores!" The words echo off the walls and strike like lightning bolts into his fragile skull.

She changes the subject. "I want you to go trolling today. We needs business, and there's no one in the basement now for a week. If this keeps up, I will be in the basement. You want that for your momma? You want for your momma to be in the basement, huh?"

"No Momma! No! No! I will go trolling. I will, I promise." He says with all the strength he can muster.

"Never forget. You are an Adamov!"

"Yes, Momma."

2

MORTUARY ALLEY—THURS.—9:43 AM

UNDER THE EAVE, OUT of the rain, Chris is leaning with his back against the brick building. One boot is on the ground and the sole of the other is on the wall. In his long duster coat, he looks like a range rider from a western movie. He's got to have a smoke before facing his Uncle Radko.

He's reaching deep into the pocket of his worn jeans, feeling for the smooth chunk of chrome metal, that is his grandfather's, WWII Zippo cigarette lighter. After a worried moment, he finds it. In one smooth move, he flips the top open with his thumb and rolls the striker across his thigh. Gold sparks fly into the fluid drenched wick. It ignites into blue and gold flame. The ionized odor of the flint, the acrid tinge of the lighter fluid and the flame flickering in his hand comfort him. He cups his palms around the lighter to protect the flame from the breeze and lights up.

Chris takes a long pull off the cigarette, inhaling the sweet smoke deeply into his lungs where he holds it for a second. With the exhale, his spine tingles and he feels the instant healing. He takes another hit then slowly exhales the blue-gray smoke into the rain falling beyond the eave. Alcohol, nicotine and cannabis are his allies in his struggle with the world and its horrible people.

Once a week, on stage, is the only place he feels safe. Comedy night is Wednesdays at Rocking Roxy's. There he hides behind the microphone in his stage persona. He can throw crap at the people all he wants and they love him for it.

"I'm a victim of circumstance. I didn't ask to be here and I'm not digging at all." That is the first nervous line that he throws to his booze sodden audience. With one hand, he shades his eyes from the spotlight and looks for them in the darkness.

"This is a horrible world," Chris mutters to himself as he snuffs the butt of his cigarette out on his boot heel. Then, with his thumb and forefinger, he twists the last little bits of chopped tobacco out of the butt, letting them fall into the rose hedge.

'It's fertilizer,' he tells himself. 'My lungs may go black but I'm helping to green the world.'

While chuckling at his own dark thinking, he rolls the soft cotton filter up and puts it in his pants pocket with a few others. Donka keeps the place inspection ready and is hysterical if anything is out of place.

Chris looks at the neighborhood he was born in and mutters to himself, 'I've got to get out of here or I won't see thirty.'

3

RADKO'S OFFICE—THURS.—10:30 AM

THE ONLY LIGHT IN THE room comes from an ancient desk lamp. Radko's there, stuffed into a cheap blue suit, his hair greased down tight with gold rings on six of his fat little fingers. He's concentrating on a shiny new, yellow wooden pencil; bouncing it repeatedly off the desk by its eraser. On the other side of the desk, in a plush, leather wing-back chair, Chris waits patiently for his nut job uncle to say something.

Radko is leaning into the task with his ear near the desktop. His little blue eyes are glistening from the dark circles that surround them. He throws the pencil again—eraser first—into the desktop and watches as it wobbles feebly into the air. He snatches it before it can fall. With each quick grab, Radko looks at Chris with a triumphant, yellow toothed, shit-eating grin.

'He must have been watching Bruce Lee videos on YouTube again.' Chris thinks to himself as he watches Radko snatch the wobbling pencil out of the air.

Framed color photographs of funerals, and shiny hearses with fancy coffins, emerge from the shadows. In one photo is a metal flake gold casket with a red flame paint job. It has chrome exhaust pipes for handles. It is surrounded by a crew of greasers frowning in sparkly gold suits.

'This is hideous. Just wrap me up and leave me on a scaffold under the endless blue sky, like a Lakota warrior. Let the ravens have me.'

"I could have been an astronaut," Radko says as he bounces the pencil again. As it lifts off the desk, he makes rocket sounds and snatches it before it can fall.

"You ever see how those rockets curve away like that after they take off? You ever notice that, Chris?"

"Yes, I have."

"Doesn't make sense, does it Chris?"

"No, it doesn't."

Radko shakes his head and drops the pencil into an old coffee cup with several others. He brings his fingertips together and looks across them at Chris with his blue raccoon eyes. "Your mother says you are drinking again, Chris."

Chris shifts nervously in his seat. "Yes, I slipped. I will go to a meeting later and get back on track today. I promise."

"I don't care if you drink Chris, except it makes your mother unhappy. Go to a meeting, just cut back and everything will be fine."

"You know, your mother and I are going to the Eternal Rest convention in Oklahoma City. We got tickets for the Last Dance Ball, the Headstone Awards, the whole kit and caboodle."

"If we get any business, just call on Tripoli's across town for embalming services. They will bill us. I really wish you would reconsider embalming school, Chris." Chris squirms in his seat.

"You still carrying that big cross around?" Radko asks.

Chris reaches deep into his duster's pocket and pulls out the big crucifix. Jesus is hanging on it—in full color—all scourged and bloody. He holds it up proudly for Radko to see. Radko winces and puts a palm up to shade his eyes. "OK, that is enough, Chris. You can put it away now." Chris puts it back carefully and pats his pocket lovingly.

"Just make your mother happy and go trolling today."

"It's ridiculous," Chris mutters to himself, trying not to laugh out loud.

"It's scientifically proven." Radko says as if the word science would validate his point. "You know the law, Chris, Nature..."

"I know," Chris interjects, "Nature abhors a vacuum. Right. I just don't believe it applies here. When you are driving somewhere alone, does your car fill with pedestrians going in your direction?"

"You have to say the words, Chris, the words. Your mother knows the words. Our guru taught her personally. We create our own reality, Chris. This is Mystical Scientism. It's not a religion. It is science." Radko adds enthusiastically. "We are the Gods, Chris! It is these false religions that have caused us so much pain and for us to lose touch with our true God like nature."

"Our Guru Puramahamasawamy Rama says: 'Through sound, energy and crystals we—'The Chosen Ones'—can transform ourselves back into the Gods that we really are. You should come to one of our meetings and see this is true, Chris. You can be chosen too, Chris. I know you can."

Chris is looking blankly at Radko. He is thinking of how his father committed suicide and his mother went nuts, shortly after Radko arrived from the old country, with this 'Mystical Scientism' nonsense.

"Polish your hearse up and go trolling. I know you have noticed how it works?"

"Coincidence."

"Your father left that hearse to you. Be proud Chris. Take it for a nice drive. Let the people in town see it. This storm will soon pass. Put on your blacks and go trolling. To me, there is nothing so relaxing as a beautiful day of trolling."

"It's dark thinking." Chris tells Radko.

"Chris, there you go with your Jesus thinking again. There is no God, no afterlife, there are no angels. What we have here is all we get unless we transform ourselves through Mystical Scientism, Chris."

"I know it is hard to find a job now and you want to have your own place, but your mother loves having you here. We just need a little help. I'm asking you to do your part for us and for your mother."

Chris knows that the money he makes driving the hearse and digging graves for Radko will never get him where he needs to go. It's like they say in Alcoholics Anonymous: 'Let go and let God.' He knows that one day soon he will move to Austin and he'll be on stage and killing it, at The Comedy Mothership. That's where he belongs and that is where his fame and fortune await.

"Oh, and one other thing before we finish here." Radko said, shifting subjects. "Mick went out to cover the grave and saw you in the hearse with another one. Chris, this has to stop." Radko said with a chuckle before adding. "He said she was a real screamer, too."

Guilt and embarrassment flash through Chris's mind and body. "She was in a bad way, grieving. We were talking. I was just consoling her and then..."

"It's one of the perks of the business, Chris," Radko interjects. "Don't worry, we've all done it. Like a bunch of vultures around here, just waiting for someone to die, so we can take the spoils. Someone's got to do it, right? Might as well be us, huh, Chris?"

Chris is ashamed, once again reminded that he is a hopeless sinner.

"Don't forget, we are going to be out of town for three or four days. You are in charge."

"I understand Uncle Radko. Everything will be fine."

The lights flicker, and the thunder rolls.

4

MORTUARY GARAGE—THURS.—11:11 AM

THE RAIN IS LETTING up, but with all the thick cloud cover; it's still dark for noon time. The garage door is open and a single yellowed lightbulb hangs from the ceiling. Chris is polishing his midnight blue Cadillac 1990 hearse.

It's painted with a dark blue metal flake that shines like stars in a moonless midnight sky. The car was customized for a rich mortician in Atlanta, who later went mad and committed unspeakable acts. The elaborate front end is all chrome, dominated by a solid-silver swept-wing angel, with a grinning skull for a face.

They found the note on the car's bench seat, after his father had shot himself. In his father's handwriting, it said that the hearse was to be Chris's or, "I will come back and haunt your asses!" Chris got the hearse and drove his father to his final resting spot in it.

It is impeccable, not a blemish or scar to be found anywhere. He had thought of selling it and getting something practical, but he's just not ready. Besides, he has his 1988 Chevy truck for transportation and the hearse provides income. Driving funerals for his mother and Radko isn't ideal, but some income is better than none.

Chris dips the polishing rag into the wide mouth of the paste can and works some of the stiff yellow paste onto his rag. "They just don't make them like they used to," he mutters to himself as he spreads the wax in perfect, uniform circles and makes his way around the big car. The metal-flake paint job with its—stars in the sky effect—reminds Chris of the soul's mysterious journey after leaving this earthly life.

Soon enough, he is waiting for the wax to dry so he can buff it out. With the humidity, it is taking longer than usual. He takes a pull off his smoke, watches the rain fall and lets his mind wander.

'Where do we go from here?' That was the big question before he was 'saved' by some Pentecostals when he was 21 and in college. Chris believes his final destination could be Heaven. But now he is a backslider, as they say, around the church. He has slid back into ways of life that are not Christian ways at all.

He had six months of sobriety under his belt before he slipped yesterday. But thank God, nothing bad had happened. At least he didn't think anything bad had happened. If something bad did happen, he would hear about it soon enough. With that thought in mind, Chris turned the sound off on his phone. When he feels like himself again, he will call Danny and ask him, 'What happened last night?'

Yesterday, when he was walking to the market, Danny rolled up alongside him and offered him a ride. Chris made the mistake of getting in. Without even thinking about it, he took a hit when Danny passed his pipe over. By the second puff, they were on their way to meet Danny's new roommate and her 'smoking hot friend' at The Horseshoe Lounge.

He must have blacked out around 11 pm. The last thing he remembered was drinking like a pirate in the poolroom and acting like an ass. He could still hear his own voice echoing, 'Life is like a pool game. There's nothing you can do about it.'

His memory of the scene was distorted like a funhouse mirror. They just weren't getting his point at all. He watched the hot girl heave her big purse over her shoulder and walk boldly out the door.

When he came to, he was face down and spread-eagled in the front yard with his phone in an outstretched hand. It was pouring down rain. Thank God his mom or Radko had not found him laying out there.

'Slips are part of getting sober. Nobody gets it right the first time,' Chris reminds himself, but he feels like a nut. He thinks of his mother's instability and remembers the adage, 'The apple doesn't fall, far from the tree.'

Chris remembers: It was a pretty spring morning. The Sun was filtering in through the silky drapes joined by a soft breeze. He and his mom and dad were enjoying their fresh, hot and fluffy pancakes with eggs. They were looking forward to a relaxing 'do nothing' kind of day.

"Nature abhors a vacuum!" She declared this with an intense, wide-eyed realization as if it had just come to her. She looked knowingly at both of them, then dug back into her pancakes and eggs without another word.

His father had a sad look on his face, as if he understood the grim consequences of Donka's realization.

By the end of the day, the 'Nature Abhors a Vacuum' law and its implications were made clear. If business was slow, just go out and drive the empty hearse around—Poof!—It is empty no more. She could not be dissuaded. She had been watching 'The Science Channel.'

Since Donka was an avid fisherman, she understood the concept of trolling, throwing a lure into the lake and motoring along slowly, dragging the lure in front of all the unsuspecting fish. With these new and sound scientific principles in mind, the empty hearse becomes a magnetic lure and the people of Willburn are just dumb fish.

Since then, whenever the money was low or there was something she really, really wanted, 'Trolling' was the order of the day.

Chris dropped his cigarette butt in the empty coffee can that he kept hidden in the rose bushes. He took a clean buffing pad off the shelf, put it on the slow rotating buffer and flicked it on. He started back around his hearse, taking the dried wax glaze off to reveal a beautiful glistening shine.

When he finished, he took the buffer pad off and threw it to an empty spot on the cluttered workbench. When the pad hit the target, the rain stopped—just like that—like someone had thrown a switch and stopped it.

Chris lights another smoke, grabs his driver's coat off the rack and leaves the old style cap hanging on its peg. He puts on the coat and searches the pockets for his black leather gloves and pulls them on. He likes the fit of the thin deerskin. It feels comforting. They're snug when he makes a fist. He checks himself in the mirror, then turns and walks to the hearse...

"Ladies and gentlemen, please give a warm welcome to The Mortician." Rapturous applause and screams of approval greet him as he steps out onto the big stage to host The Academy Awards ceremony. He is reaching for the microphone and thousands are applauding him when...

He swings the hearse door open and drops onto the soft leather bench seat. He pumps the pedal twice and turns the key. The engine coughs so he taps the gas pedal. Then comes the warm and steady rumble of a big old gasoline engine. Chris has the feeling that he is about to do something wrong, but how can he be? This trolling for bodies is crazy nonsense. He makes the sign of the cross on himself, just in case. The he puts her in gear and pulls out of the garage and onto the long concrete driveway.

As he slowly rolls down the narrow driveway, he glances up at the attic room. Donka is there at the window, backed by the warm glowing candlelight. He can see her lips moving. She is 'Saying the Words' and looking out over the city. He checks to his right and is relieved to find his Bible on the seat near him. He pulls it tight to his thigh and pats it. "This is not my idea," he says to the Mother Mary figurine praying on the dashboard.

He hits the button to roll the windows down. Mrs. Watson's evil black cat is sitting eye level in the bougainvilleas that drape the wall all the way to the street. As Chris gets close, the cat arches her back and hisses, showing her fangs to him. She's wild-eyed, glaring through the windshield as he creeps slowly toward her. Wondering for just a moment if she is rabid and might spring through the open window to shred his face, Chris hits the button and rolls the window up.

The cat drifts safely past and into the rear-view mirror. He rolls the window back down and rests his elbow on the doorsill. As the hearse meets the sidewalk, a Chihuahua hurls itself against its reflection in the hubcap. The owner pulls the dog back on its leash and gives Chris a filthy look as he floats onto the street.

He turns left toward downtown. It will take a while to cross the business district. Then he will pass into the more 'well to do' residential areas on the other side. Wealthy people want the more expensive coffins, urns, headstones and they rent fancy limos. The westside is the perfect place to troll for the big fish.

5

TROLLING—THURS.—1:03 PM

CHRIS IS TRAPPED IN traffic, following close behind a dirty city bus when he sees a woman leaning out of the bus shelter up ahead.

He feels himself tighten up. 'Oh, my god it's her.'

Just a couple of days before, he was at the corner waiting for the light to change. With earbuds in his ears and his boot soles on the curb's edge, he was leaning into life, like a dog on a leash. As he watched the thick traffic flow, Chris rocked to the train-track rhythm of Johnny Cash's 'Cocaine Blues.' Right when Johnny sang the part—'and I shot that bad bitch down'—she came around the corner riding shotgun, in a red convertible sports car, with the top down. Her girlfriend was at the wheel. They were laughing and the music was loud. She was holding her right hand up into the breeze as they made the turn. The little car was getting so close that Chris was easing back, but then she looked up at him and he saw the laughter in her eyes. Without thinking, he reached out to touch her hand, but her friend shouted something and she turned away just as they sped past.

As the bus slows to a stop, she steps to the curb and waits, killing it in heels, a short black skirt and a white silk blouse. She's carrying a well-worn guitar case.

'She's built like a ballet dancer, maybe 23 or 24?' Chris whispers to himself. Then she takes a step up and disappears into the bus. If he wasn't driving the hearse, he would pull ahead to the next stop and get on the bus 'to investigate the situation.' He takes a deep hit off his cigarette and considers the options.

Like a giant turtle, the bus pushes away from the curb and continues on its way. Chris follows, but before too long, the big orange arrow flasher signals for a right turn. Chris' heart drops as the bus churns and smokes its way around the corner. He knows he will probably never see her again.

He almost follows, but pauses when he remembers his poor mother. Filled with regret, Chris pushes on the gas and continues straight ahead, across the busy intersection. Leaning on the wheel, he's staring blankly ahead as she fills imagination. He is dangerously oblivious to the world and all the traffic moving around him.

"Fuck it," he says and flicks his cigarette out the open window. He spins the big steering wheel hard left. The big car comes around clockwise like a 6,000 pound steel bull demanding his space. Horns blare and tires squeal all around. The hearse's silver skulled angel is sweating and praying to God, as it sweeps just past the window of the platter-eyed boomer in his Jaguar.

This deadly merry-go-round of flashing colors, screeching tires, and honking horns lasts only a couple of seconds. Then somehow, Chris ends up right back where he was, behind the bus. Trembling, he makes the sign of the cross, adjusts the rear-view mirror and looks for the law.

When the bus slows for its next stop, he passes it and races ahead. A few blocks down, he pulls into a public parking lot. Luckily, he finds a spot. "Thank you, God! This is meant to be," he assures himself as he gets out and runs to the bus shelter.

Leaning on the shelter wall, Chris is calming his breath and watching the bus approach.

"I wish my job was that interesting," says the old man sitting there on the bench.

"Me too." Chris agrees.

"Must be for a woman, then."

Chris just nods.

"Good luck," says the man, shaking his head.

"She's beautiful." Chris says as he walks to the curb to meet the bus.

The old man slaps his knee and laughs, "That makes it worse!"

Chris is looking at him and trying to think of what to say; then he hears the bus brakes lock and the doors clatter open behind him.

Inside, it's a full house. People of every shape, size, color and description fill the interior. Thankfully, the windows are open and a fresh breeze of rain-washed air is flowing through.

She's halfway down the aisle on the right, reading a magazine. There are only a few empty seats, but the one across the aisle from her is empty.

'Thank you Lord! This is definitely meant to be,' Chris repeats to himself.

As the bus jerks into motion, Chris steadies himself by grabbing the passenger rail hanging from the ceiling. He follows it down the aisle, dropping quietly onto the empty seat across from her. His eyes land first on her hands and trimmed, natural fingernails. The short black skirt and high heels accentuate her tanned and toned legs. She is reading, 'TV Celebrities' magazine. As she turns the pages, she whispers the words to herself. This is the most attractive woman Chris has ever seen.

'Maybe she is a soccer player?' Chris thinks to himself.

He can see her plain as day on the field. Her ponytail is flying as she kicks the impossible winning goal. Then later they are walking hand in hand after a movie. He stops her under the marquee lights and kisses her full lips. Just as their tongues touch, she pushes him away. "Come on, cowboy. We're not married yet," she says with a promising smile and deep burning passion in her big brown eyes.

A siren screams by under the bus' windows and brings Chris back to the present moment.

"You like the entertainment industry?" Chris blurts out. She looks at him cocked eyed and waits. Chris melts under her gaze.

"I'm a comedian," he adds with immediate and cosmic regret.

"Oh...I see." She responds with a patient smile.

"You a musician?" he asks, trying to recover his composure.

"I'm a singer songwriter," she says, as if no one has ever spoken those magical words before. She looks him up and down again, then returns her attention to the magazine.

He was toast, and they both knew it. Chris was staring out the dirty front windows, flush with embarrassment, when the bus lurched to a stop. She gets up and drops the magazine back onto the seat with a dismissal that only a lot of money or a beautiful young woman can get away with. As she reaches for the guitar case, something catches Chris' eye: 'ZOIE—Willburn—Texas' is stenciled in white on the black case guitar case.

"Bye," she says with a wave over her shoulder as she heads down the aisle toward the exit.

"Take it easy," is the best Chris can manage.

She stops and looks back at him. "You're so cute," she says with a shrug and a sigh. Then she just turns and continues away down the aisle..

He slides over to the empty window seat and looks for her. Just then, she steps out onto the curb. She must have read his mind because she looks right at him like he's a creepy window peeper.

She was meeting a guy that Chris had seen around town. She fell into his arms and whispered something in his ear as they walked away, arm in arm. Without looking back, the guy flipped Chris the bird over his shoulder. Just then, the bus jerked away from the curb, causing Chris to smack his forehead on the window. He fell back onto his seat, rubbing his forehead. "Asshole," Chris muttered under his breath.

"You've been outclassed, boy," a woman's syrupy southern voice said from behind him.

Chris looked over the seat-back to see who was talking to him. It was a little old black lady. A newspaper was crumpled in her bony hands.

"You be careful. You can't move that girl. She'll break your heart. She's a whore!"

"Sorry?" he asked, trying to buy himself some time.

"You got to know when to quit. Like the song says, 'You gotta know when to hold'em and know when to fold'em.' He's a rich one, that boy. But with all that money he's got? He ain't no better than her. He's a senator's son. Those drugs and all? He gets arrested? His daddy just gets him out like nothing ever happened. Everybody knows it. Demon possessed! They's all demon possessed, I say. Mother, fuck those people! I know. I know I need to go to church, but a woman can only take so much. You need a good girl, not some whore like that one."

With that, she disappeared back behind her newspaper. Chris was stunned. He stared at the wall of newsprint in front of him, relieved that he did not have to respond.

At the next stop, he gets off, crosses the street and takes the first bus back to where he had parked. Then with the windows down, he smoked cigarettes and trolled the most luxurious neighborhoods in town and tried to forget the whole thing.

Chris checks his watch. It is nearly 2 pm when he pulls into 'Crazy Burger.' He gets a double burger with fries to go and heads for Confederate Park. It is a little park next to Thompson Elementary. There's hardly ever any people around. He can eat in solitude at one of the picnic tables and catch a nap in the back of the hearse.

When he gets to the park, he glides to a stop on the left, puts it in park, and turns the engine off. The silence is soft and welcoming. The kids must still be in class. On his left is the elementary school and the park, with lush green grass and warm speckled light filtering through the trees. On his right is a cozy neighborhood. A chain-link fence is all that divides the school from the park. It is like the school is in the park. When he was a kid, there was no fence, but that was a long time ago.

Chris is disappointed to see that the lawn sprinklers are running and the tables are soaked. He is going to have to eat in the car.

As he spreads the french fries out on the paper bag they came in, he sees a big black raven standing on the sidewalk, looking at him. Chris tosses him part of a french fry. Another raven drops in from above, landing right next to the first one.

Chris chews his burger and shares his fries with the growing crowd of ravens. He's amazed at the size of them.

'Good thing they aren't any bigger,' Chris thinks to himself.

After finishing his lunch, Chris takes a walk around the park. It is a truly magical day, very quiet, and no one else is around to be seen. He stops to watch a snail trace its way across the sidewalk to the grass. Chris is worrying that someone will step on the poor guy when he hears an unfamiliar sound behind him. It's a scraping sound. When he turns around to look, he finds to his horror that he is facing a giant sized, shiny black raven. It must be eight feet tall. It's looking at him cockeyed.

The raven takes one hop, then with its beak, it snatches Chris up by his ankle. It whips him repeatedly onto the sidewalk—until he is blood soaked and red—just like a French fry with ketchup.

Chris is struggling to open one of those stupid little ketchup packets when he hears the racket coming from the school grounds. It is the school band. They come around the corner of a building sounding terrible. It is a real cacophony.

'They are so young,' Chris thinks, 'They must be about ten years old.'

Chris doesn't see a teacher with them. A few Boy Scouts in tan uniforms are mock goose-stepping ahead of the band. The whole formation is heading toward the flagpole.

As this patriotic scene plays out in front of him, Chris enjoys his lunch and continues to share bits with the ravens. It takes little to please them. Soon there is a large crowd of the black birds around and on the hearse.

The Boy Scouts march to the base of the flagpole and come to attention. One boy steps out of the band's formation, raises his horn to his lips and 'squeaks' through his own version of Reveille. After a moment of reverent silence, the band attempts the Star-Spangled Banner. The Boy Scouts lower the flag and fold it into a perfect triangle. Then they all march back toward the school.

Chris crumples his lunch, wrapping the paper into a tight ball. "Sorry, you all," he says to the ravens as he shows them his empty palms. Then he leans out the window and tosses the ball over their heads toward a distant city trash can. Like a crowd at a tennis match, they watch the ball arc through the air. Chris knows he will have to get out and pick up the scattered paper when it explodes into a mess on the sidewalk. It was a combination of laziness and curiosity that made him try it.

The ball begins to drop toward the pavement several feet short of the can. Chris is reaching for the door handle to go clean up, but stops when he sees the ball hovering in midair. Then it is suddenly sucked into the can's mouth, like a paper ball into the nozzle of a powerful vacuum cleaner.

The ravens turn as one. They look to Chris for the answer.

6

A. A. MEETING—THURS.—5:50 PM

THIS MEETING OF ALCOHOLICS Anonymous is held every evening at 6 pm, on the ground floor of an old office building. It's in the shadow of a busy freeway overpass. Chairs are placed arm to arm and shoved tight against the four walls. They surround a dozen rows of people who face towards the man sitting on a couch at the long end of the room. He's running the meeting. The 'Twelve Steps' and 'Twelve Traditions,' printed in black and white, hang like sacred scrolls on the wall behind him.

The clock on the wall says it's 5:55 pm and the room is already full. People are poking their heads in the door, scanning for a seat, then heading to one of the overflow rooms down the hall.

They come by the hundreds, battle scarred and broken-hearted. They are the weary veterans and survivors from wars of their own creation.

The room, painted a soothing powder blue, is lit only by mismatched table lamps located around the periphery. Chris finds comfort in the warm, low light coming from the old lamps. He got in early and grabbed his favorite place. Slouched against the back wall, he's drinking coffee from a 12 oz. Styrofoam cup. It is hot, strong, and loaded with powdered creamer and sugar.

A big Native American man with long hair and a black leather jacket drops heavily onto the couch next to Chris. Involved in his coffee, Chris does not look to see who just sat next to him.

"I heard you was shit faced down at the Horseshoe Lounge last night. Is that right Chris?"

Chris immediately recognizes the voice and cautiously turns his head just enough to see Henri, his A.A. sponsor. It is Henri's job to guide Chris as he works through the Twelve Steps to recovery. Chris truly regrets that he picked Henri to be his sponsor. Henri is a tough, no bullshit kind of guy. Chris would rather he had no sponsor, but the court demanded it as part of his probation for his DUI conviction. The conviction that neither Radko or his mother know anything about.

"Yeah, I'm sorry Henri. I fucked up," he says as he looks back into his cup, wishing he could crawl into it and hide there.

As Chris tries to take a nonchalant sip, Henri slaps him on the sternum with the back of his big knuckled hand. The jolt splashes coffee all over and turns Chris' body into putty. He gasps for breath.

"You're going to be at the ceremony tomorrow, right Chris?"

"Yeah—yeah, I'll be there. I promise," Chris says, trying to pull himself together.

Henri leans really close and whispers into his ear. "If you ain't there Chris, I promise," Henri says, crossing himself and nodding his head before continuing, "I will find you in whatever shithole you've crawled into and beat the hell out of you."

"OK Henri. OK, I promise I'm sorry, really. I just…"

Henri just pats him on the knee and gets up. He goes over to another young man, who greets Henri with a smile and a handshake.

Henri is a minister at a native christian church. Chris had promised Henri before to be at one of his ceremonies and blew it off to go get high. Henri said the ceremony would help Chris overcome his addictions and other problems. Chris is concerned because Henri is a man of his word.

"Welcome to the West Town open meeting of Alcoholics Anonymous. I'm Bill and I'm an alcoholic," the meeting leader shouts out.

"Hi Bill!" the room responds as one voice.

7

ROCKING ROXY'S—THURS.—9:00 PM

IN THE MERCILESS WHITE light of the spotlight, Chris is holding his crucifix up high. He shades his eyes with his free hand and talks into the microphone, on the stand, in front of him.

Chris is the new guy, so he is up first. The room is dark and nearly empty, with only a smattering of people. Later, the place will be packed. His routine had gone so much better, in his bedroom in front of the mirror. The spotlight is right in his eyes, so he can't see the audience at all. His bit about vampire school is going over like a belly flop at the Olympic Games.

"This sucks." A man's booze sodden voice interrupts. "Me and my girl here need some laughs."

"Yeah, say something funny, honey. It's OK we all been there," the woman adds.

Chris swallows, adjusts his fake vampire teeth, and starts again. "Yeah, like I was saying the other night, I went for a hike in the moonlight and…"

"Aw shut up," another insists vehemently. "Get the hook and get him out of here!" This alone gets laughs from the audience.

"OK then," Chris responds feebly, "Feeling a little pent up, huh? Maybe you need a transfusion, huh?!"

"Go fuck yourself!" The voice responds.

Two doormen come down the hallway from the rear and remove the drunk. They drag him from the room, crossing right in front of the stage as they go.

"See?" Chris laughs at him. "See what happens when you are an asshole?"

Chris holds his crucifix out at the man. "Get thee behind me, Satan," he declares while making the sign of the cross and they drag the drunk away.

The manager comes out from behind the curtains and whispers into Chris' ear. "Your time is up, Chris." He takes the microphone from Chris and pats him on the shoulder. "Yes, ladies and gents, let's give a warm hand to—The Mortician."

No one claps as Chris steps off the stage. The next comic coming up is a woman. They pass on the steps.

"I loved your bit, Chris. You are great," she says with a snicker. "Keep it up."

"Thanks, Madge." Chris responds as he heads for the restroom. There he throws up, washes his face and checks himself in the mirror, before taking a seat at the empty bar.

8

MORTUARY RECEPTION ROOM—FRI.—11:00 AM

RADKO AND DONKA ARE coming down the stairs. Radko's 'Sacred Order of the Coffin Cheaters' pendant is bouncing off his belly, one step at a time, as their luggage tumbles down behind them.

"Now you remember, Honey, we will be back in five days. If you need any help, just call Tripoli's across town OK, Honey?" Then she added sweetly, "We've told them that you are alone here and they understand."

Radko chimed in, "You be sure to keep this place locked up. Those formaldehyde thieves are everywhere now."

"I know. I will."

"I found one smoking it—in the alley yesterday morning—when I took the trash out," Radko said then continued, "I got a shot off at him with my slingshot but missed him. I'll get him next time."

"OK, OK. It will be fine, I promise."

Donka perches on her tiptoes to kiss her son on the forehead. Chris grabs his mom's bags and helps her down the stairs to the street. They hug and she cries. Radko just nods and fires up the car. They pull away with a final wave.

Chris is reaching for the doorknob when he hears the brakes of the city bus squealing to a stop. It is rare for the bus to stop out front of the funeral home. He pauses to see what is going on. With a clatter and a flop, the bus door opens and Zoie steps into the warm sunlight. She's wearing big dark sunglasses and is dressed impeccably in black, from the top of her perfect bangs to the tip of her pointy, high-gloss shoes. She Looks like a Hollywood movie star in mourning.

As the bus doors close and the giant machine rolls away belching smoke and haze, Zoie pulls an ivory handkerchief from her purse. She dabs her eyes and blows her nose.

Chris pulls the door open, steps inside and closes the door behind him. He pulls the lace curtains aside on the window bordering the door and peers out to see which way she goes.

Zoie is looking up at the wooden sign hanging above the entrance. "Adamov Mortuary," she whispers as she reads the words to herself. She puts the handkerchief back in her purse, then mounts the concrete stairs that lead up to the entrance.

The sign on the door has a yellow 'Sad Face' on it that reads, 'Please Come In.'

She twists the solid-brass knob, and pushes the heavy wooden door open. The little brass bells hanging on the door tinkle, as Chris slips out of the room.

"Someone will be right there," he shouts from the hall, wishing he had locked the front door and bought himself more time to think.

"Yes, of course," Zoie replies with a sniffle. She takes off her sunglasses and puts them in her cavernous purse. While she is elbow deep in her purse, Chris slips back into the room and takes a seat at the reception desk behind her. He leans way back in the chair and puts his feet up on the desk.

"Oh, damn it." She says in frustration as she scans the room. Eventually she turns and her eyes fall on Chris. A look of horror crosses her face, as if she has spotted a giant cockroach.

"It's the comedian." She thinks out loud.

This is not the response Chris had hoped for.

"What's going on here? Is this some kind of joke?" She shouts as Chris tries to pull himself together.

"No—you're Zoie right?" Chris says.

"Is this a hidden camera TV show?"

"No," he says finally standing, holding his palms up trying to calm her, "I work here, I mean...we live here. I mean...my mother and my Uncle Radko own the place."

In desperation, he grabs a fresh, well-puffed box of Kleenex from the desk and holds it out to her. She pauses and looks at it with deep suspicion, but then quickly snatches a few sheets. While she dabs her eyes and nose Chris gently guides her to an ornate couch. It rests under a massive, framed oil painting of an expensive coffin and flower arrangement.

"But you said you were a comedian."

"It's a long story."

"You must be a pretty lousy comedian."

Zoie drops onto the couch and sobs into her palms, "My fiancé is dead!"

He is elated, but catches himself just as he feels a broad smile cross his face. He manages to look really sad before she looks back up at him. He can put on a real sad face if he has to. It is part of the trade and a family tradition.

'Thank you, God!' Chris thinks to himself.

"Oh Zoie, that is terrible! What happened?" Chris says. He seems so sympathetic.

"He was just standing at the window, watching the school children take down the flag."

"Where do you live, Zoie?" Chris asks her cautiously.

"We live right across the street from Thompson Elementary near Confederate Park...you know?"

"Yes," Chris whispers as he suddenly feels weak, like his soul is detaching from his body.

Zoie continues, "Then he said, 'It's such a beautiful day. Look Baby, the kids are taking down the American flag. It is such a wonderful flag.' Then he says, 'What are all those ravens doing on that car? It gives me the creeps.' I looked and saw a big black car there, like an old station wagon, and there were ravens all over and all around it. Anyway, a man leans out the window and throws a ball of paper toward the trash can. 'No way,' Warren said, as it flew. He's a big basketball fan. I didn't think it would ever make it either, but it kind of got sucked right into the can. It was weird the way it did that. One of those impossible shots. You know? I looked at Warren, like we were together watching a basketball game on TV. He had this wide eyed, shocked look on his face like he was amazed too, right? And then, he grabs his chest, croaks twice and falls face first into my brand new glass coffee table."

A tsunami of guilt sweeps over Chris. "Oh, my God. I am so sorry, Zoie. I'm so sorry," he says and he means it.

"It's not your fault. I tried to get him up, but he was all cut up, bloody and too heavy. I ran downstairs and got a neighbor to help. He's a paramedic. He checked him and performed CPR until the ambulance arrived. Nothing they could do." She looked baffled and cried again, harder than ever.

"Warren was so handsome and kind. He was so good to me."

"The ambulance people took him away from me." She said sadly.

"Would you like for us to make arrangements for you, Zoie?" It was all Chris could think of to say. He knew that his involvement could not be proven. It was not possible anyway.

"Yes," she answered.

Chris pulled his phone out. Shaking, he hit a familiar button to ring the morgue.

"I will have... what was his name?" His voice trembled as he asked her.

"Warren."

"I will have Warren's remains brought here. They should be here by tomorrow. This will give you a little time to rest before we proceed with the necessities."

"OK" was all she could manage.

"How will you get home? You shouldn't drive."

"I took the bus here. I can take it back."

"Let me drive you."

"You are so kind, Chris. I am sorry I misjudged you. You are a good man."

Zoie steps over to Chris. She puts her arms around him, buries her face in his neck and sobs. Chris feels like he is dreaming and comforts her the best he can as his guilt washes away.

'Thank God that son of a bitch is dead.' He thinks to himself and realizes the truth, 'I am a very bad man.'

Zoie leans back, looks deeply into his eyes, then kisses him gently and fully. His whole being ignites. They melt into each other as the phone falls to the floor.

Later...

They are spent, and the place is ruined. The antique couch's legs are broken and it is tilting like the Titanic sinking into an ocean of lush carpet.

In their passion, oblivious to the damage, they had continued on the floor. There in wild abandon, Zoie pulled the tall curtains down on top of them. When finally spent, they slept like the dead, only to awaken like remorseful drunks from a very bad binge.

Embarrassed, Zoie wraps herself in the curtains to cover her nakedness, while Chris hides behind the broken down couch and pulls his briefs back on.

She is looking around the room with her hand over her mouth, like she has never seen it before.

"Take me home?" She pleads trembling as he puts his shirt on.

"Of course." Chris says, not looking at her.

He drives her to her place in his truck. It is a quiet ride over. They have been taken by a force they cannot control.

"I don't know what came over me," she says, crying softly. "I love Warren and I want my Warren back."

She is obviously mentally disturbed, but Chris is in love.

When they get to her house, he parks near where he was, when he watched the Boy Scouts take the flag down.

"That is our place up there," she says, pointing to the upstairs window.

Chris sees the big picture window overlooking the schoolyard. He remembers having lunch with the ravens—right there—across the street from her house. He gets out and goes around to open her door.

"You're not going to embalm him too soon, are you?" She asks as she gets out.

"Too soon?" Chris wonders. "No, not right away. Why?"

"Oh, I don't know."

"Thank you, Chris." She takes his hand and looks into his eyes. "Can we just be friends? You are a really good guy. I need you, but I still love Warren."

"Of course, Zoie." Chris says playing along.

She kisses him lightly on the cheek, then walks away, down the sidewalk toward her front door.

"Would you like for me to pick you up?" Chris shouts hopefully.

"No, I like buses," was her simple response. "Is 6 pm tomorrow OK? I need some rest."

"Yes, of course." Chris says. He would agree to anything she said right now.

Chris watches her walk away and remembers vividly what she was like when they were naked and together.

As her door closes, Chris remembers his commitment to Henri. He checks his watch. There is no way he can make it there in time.

9

DESERT HIGHWAY—FRI.—7:03 PM

CHRIS IS AT THE WHEEL of his truck with the windows rolled down. He's flying down a desolate two-lane highway southwest of Willburn. It's getting late and he's starting to worry that he will not find the place at all. He steps on the gas when he thinks of the mess back home. He'll have to figure it out after the ceremony tonight.

'There it is!' It's an American flag draped on the barbed-wire fence, just like Henri told him it would be. Breathing a sigh of relief, he eases on the brakes, downshifts and drops off the asphalt onto the dry dirt road. It takes him straight through an opening and into the endless rolling, green and gray hills of sage and creosote.

The road is solid but sandy on top. As the truck squirms and rumbles on the washboard surface, Chris dodges the deepest ruts and the sandy pools at the edges.

He doubts that the ceremony will help him cope with the world. He has never been sober. Chris has been high every day since he was fourteen.

A couple of miles into the brush, something strange is surfacing from the scrub ahead. As he gets closer, he realizes it is the roof of an old single-wide trailer home. Used tires are scattered across the top of it.

'They are holding the roof down,' Chris realizes just as the road quickly ends. He finds himself in a clearing with the trailer and a few cars parked off to the side. The trailer looks ancient, like someone worked it over with a mallet.

"This has got to be the wrong place." Chris wonders out loud to himself, as he stops to look at the strange scene around him.

About half a dozen mutts kick up the dust, running, barking and snarling toward the truck. He rolls up his window before they can get there and leans over to crank the passenger side up too, then looks out through the dust covered windows and bug spattered windscreen.

At the edge of the parking area stands a big wooden cross with a group of men and a small fire. Henri is with them.

Chris is relieved. He eases his truck into the line of cars parked at the edge of the clearing, and looks back toward the men around the fire. Henri is coming over, calling the dogs off.

"You're late. Shut it down and come on or we're going to start without you," Henri says sharply just as Chris is rolling his window down. "Just follow me and everything will be alright," he adds before turning and walking back to the group.

Chris shuts the engine down, jumps out and dusts himself off. He glances at them. They are sizing him up. There's something about them he can't pin. Then he sees it in their faces. They are refugees from a once great land.

Behind them and up the hill is a tipi with crossed poles sticking out the top. It's just like the Plains Indians would have had, except this one is covered in canvas, not buffalo skins.

Chris realizes he is a stranger, in a strange land. He catches up with Henri, who is taking off his shirt. "Strip down to your underwear. Just hang everything on the fence there." Henri says as he points to the barbed-wire. Chris does as he is told, then follows Henri over to the tipi. Henri sits down cross-legged in the line that is forming on the ground near the door. Two men sit at the front of the line with animal-skin drums in their laps. Chris lands right behind Henri, facing the mountains in the distance. The Sun is setting there.

The last of the group finds their place in line just as the Sun touches the mountains. The drummers pound the drums frantically while the singers shriek and wail in an ancient way. This is all strange but somehow it is deeply familiar to Chris. He feels a call from the ancient past and wonders where it will take him. Closing his eyes, he lets his imagination wander into the songs.

Pictures and scenes of forgotten things he cannot identify or describe appear and disappear in his interior world. Chris opens his eyes to check his grasp of the familiar world. The Sun has passed over the mountains. What remains of daylight is shredded on the horizon. The jagged mountain tops are rimmed in molten fire. Remnants of blue sky are but patches surrounded with copper, gold and turquoise. A flock of birds in silhouette dance and shift direction with lightning speed, synchronized in the last golden rays of sunlight. While the stars shine in the firmament above, Chris closes his eyes and returns to the inner world.

After a while, the singers stop. Chris opens his eyes. The group is getting up. One by one, they bend at the waist to enter the low door of the tipi. Chris jumps up and follows Henri inside. They go clockwise around the fire, forming a circle, and sit cross-legged facing the flames. The last man in closes the flap and the circle is complete. Chris likes the feel of the firm, cool earth underneath him.

The ten men are surrounded by flickering shadows of themselves—moving and conversing on the canvas—stretched taut all around and above them.

Across the flames from Chris sits a shrunken old man. He's just skin and bones, with two long braids of silver hair and the gray eyes of a wolf. Chris turns away from his penetrating glance. Then the old man looks into Chris and says, "We are here in the belly of Mother and Father to thank them for all the blessings they have bestowed on us."

"The Roadman is dedicating this ceremony to you Chris." Henri whispers into his ear as the Roadman continues, "This ceremony is for our friend Chris, who has trouble with the white man's water and corrupted herbs. We ask our Father to clear his mind and soul and give him his woman, so he can be a whole man and fulfill his task here in this world."

The old man reaches into the beaten and rusty galvanized bucket that is sitting in front of him. It has a worn sticker on it advertising 'Abe's Hardware.'

He takes out a dried peyote button and holds it in his palm. "This is our ally Mescilito," the old man says. "He will take us to our healing if we are strong enough for the journey."

"Watch and just do what I do." Henri whispers into Chris' ear.

The drummer begins a solid, rapid beat. Chris is covered in chills from head to toe. He wants to run, but there are three men between him and the door. He sits tight and digs his fingernails into the cool damp earth.

The old man passes the bucket of buttons clockwise and picks up one of two ceramic bowls that are in front of him. He dips the button into it before passing it on. Then he takes the other bowl, dips the button in it and passes it on.

Henri sees the baffled look on Chris' face and whispers, "The first bowl is gravy and the other has flour in it. You'll see." Henri places a finger to his lips. The old man puts the button in his mouth and chews while the drummer drums.

Chris has the feeling that the lodge has somehow left Earth and is out in space. There are no windows to prove differently.

Eventually, the bucket makes its way to Henri. He takes a button out and holds it up for Chris to see. "Don't look, just take the first one you feel. That is the one that's meant for you." He says and hands him the bucket.

Chris takes the old galvanized bucket and reaches in. Just as he feels the bark like texture of a peyote button touch his fingertips—he realizes he is looking into the Roadman's eyes. He grabs the button and examines it to escape the penetrating gaze. As he passes the bucket on, Henri is dipping his button into the first bowl that has come to him. He passes that bowl to Chris, saying, "Gravy." Chris takes the bowl and dips his button in, feeling the warmth of the gravy on his fingertips. When the next bowl comes, Henri dips in and passes to Chris. "Flour," he says. Chris dips his gravy soaked button in the flour and passes the bowl on. He waits with his gravy and flour draped button in hand to see how Henri eats his. Henri pops the button into his mouth and chews, giving Chris a wizard's gluttonous smile.

Chris puts the little button into his mouth and chews. He immediately understands the reason for the flour and the gravy. The flavor is revolting. Wincing, he chews and barely chokes it down before looking back at Henri. This process continues until they have eaten 20 buttons and Henri tells him to stop.

"When you feel sick, there is a bucket behind you." Henri says as he jerks his thumb over his shoulder.

"When I feel sick?" Chris looks back into the shadows and sees a filthy red plastic bucket. He wonders just what he has gotten himself into.

As he looks around the lodge, a powerful moment from the past fills his mind. It is dreamy and light is flickering through the trees. He is in the back of the hearse with a very beautiful and very young woman. She is the sister of a man they just buried. "You look so much like him. Come here," she demands.

Chris knew it was wrong.

The old man looks across the flames at Chris and smiles knowingly. Chris looks into the crystalline gray eyes of the Roadman and realizes that he can see everything in him. He feels filthy. The old man sees him doing the same thing with a string of women and some are not so young. He knows what Chris is and Chris knows he knows. There is nowhere to run. A powerful desire for a drink of vodka sweeps over Chris. The Roadman laughs and Chris' body begins to hum. The laughter returns an echo from far beyond this sacred lodge, glowing orange under the star-filled sky.

Chris checks his watch. "Give me your watch," Henri says. Chris hands it over. Henri tosses it into the darkness behind them. Chris is now completely separated from the world and everything he knew about it.

Henri's staring out of the fire hole at the top of the lodge. The hum Chris feels comes from everywhere. It is a strange but comforting, familiar energy. The world seems more alive now than ever before.

Chris follows Henri's gaze and looks out through the fire hole as the lodge fades away. He has never seen so many stars before.

When he looks down, he is in a circle of hunters from his clan. One is Henri, who is weeping desperately. The others he does not recognize. The Moon is nestled in a river of stars flowing on the mountain's ridge. The warm firelight flickers and dances gently.

A battle scarred young warrior is sitting straight across from Chris. He is wearing buckskins and a deerskin vest decorated with colored beads and feathers. There is a white cross carved from bone hanging around his neck.

He stands up and signals for Chris to follow him. As if magnetized, Chris follows him into the scrub covered plain. The man's muscular frame ripples in the moonlight as he walks. He looks back at Chris. "I came here to take you where you need to go," he says.

Chris is captured by the perfect beauty of the world around him. The land morphs from grassy to dry and rocky as they ascend to a hilltop. The rising Sun is gigantic on the horizon and lifting slowly into the sky.

"Look there," the warrior points his arm straight into the rising Sun, "an innocent man is suffering, Chris."

Chris shields his eyes to see what he is pointing at. His eyes tear from the brilliance of the light. But then, he sees what the warrior was pointing at. Jesus Christ is hanging on the cross composed of living gold. His crown of thorns is composed of a knotted chain of ancient Hebrew letters. His endless wounds flow bloody and crimson red. When a hot and dry wind comes, some letters loosen in the crown of thorns and some are blown away.

As Chris looks into the eyes of the Lord, his own life history plays out before him in vivid detail. It is an apocalypse of inhuman behavior. Unable to face himself and what he has done, he drops like a puppet without a master. As his knees strike the earth, the whole of existence quakes and trembles.

"I'm so sorry!" he cries from the depths of his being. "I'm so sorry," he repeats again and again. All the scenes from his sordid past are flashing before him like a high-speed movie.

Remorse devours him, but when his forehead meets the ground, forgiveness comes. It is forgiveness beyond expression. He is forgiven, even for things he did not know that he needed to be forgiven for.

When he opens his eyes, it is morning. Chris sits up, brushing the sand and pebbles from his face. The tipi, about fifty yards away, is rimmed in gold against the blue sky. The Sun is coming up on the other side of it.

10

FATHER DEMETRIUS' GARDEN—SAT.—10:00 AM

CHRIS IS BACK ON THE highway, headed for home. It is a beautiful morning. He is loving the fresh morning air. Chris feels like he is connected to everything that is good in the whole world. When he woke up, no one else was to be found. The parking area was empty except for his truck.

He lights a smoke and checks his speed at 80. The limit is 75. No self respecting trooper would tag him for just 5 over the limit. Looking in the mirror, he sees a couple of pebbles and sand still impressed on his cheek. He brushes it off. There is still a slight hum in his body but his mind is tack sharp. Everything is in perfect, colorful focus. It is like his eyes have never really seen before.

By the time he gets to the edge of town, he's starving. He pulls into the 'The Smokehouse' drive thru for a brisket sandwich, some onion rings and an extra large sweet tea. He's waiting in line behind a van full of hippies, when his phone trembles on the seat next to him. It is the calendar reminding him of his monthly appointment. 'Confession with Father

Demetrius,' it says. If he misses it, he will hear about it from his mother and he is in enough trouble already. When he gets to the drive-thru window, he orders the same thing for Father Demetrius.

Chris and the Father are relaxing and eating in the rectory garden, surrounded by flowering bushes. They watch the many hummingbirds come and go as they finish their meal.

"I am still worried about my mother, Father Demetrius. You know she left 'The Way' years ago when Radko came over from Romania and got her involved with that weird teacher and my dad died like that..." Demetrius is listening closely and nodding his head. He is very familiar with the story. Chris continues, "She does a ceremony or something, up in the attic. She won't let me up there because I am not a believer. What is going on, Father? I don't know what to do! Is this evil?"

"I know, Christian, I know. You have done what you can. I will do a special 40-day service for her. That will help, but we may need to consider an exorcism."

"Exorcism! What?"

"Yes, Christian. It may have gone that far. You should move out of the house and get away from those dark practices. What about your uncle, Radko? Any progress there?"

"No... He is not a believer. He watches television all day, eats Cheetos and talks about going back to the old country. Sometimes he goes bowling."

Father Demetrius responds slowly. "Way back in 1750, Father Cosmos said, 'One day the Devil will put himself in a box and you will put it in your favorite spot in the entire house and from there, he will scream at you. His horns will go through the roof.' Chris, you should pay attention to what Father Cosmos is saying."

Chris is not really listening. "I am, but I'm lonely, Father. I am tired of walking 'The Way' alone."

"You are still in the woods. You are getting closer to 'The Way,' but you must stop taking drugs, drinking, and having premarital sex. There are many good boys in Hell, yes?"

"I try, Father, I really do, but..."

"There can be no buts on the 'Judgement Day,' Christian. Me...even Father Demetrius, I cannot be assured of entry into our Father's glorious kingdom. I try to pray without ceasing, for his Mercy."

"Pray without ceasing, Father?"

"Yes, The Jesus Prayer!"

"Oh right. Sorry, Father. I wasn't thinking."

"Christian! You must pay attention every moment. Watch your thoughts constantly and strive to pray unceasingly."

"I know, Father, I know, but my thoughts are horrible. That is why..."

"Lord Jesus Christ, Son of God, have mercy on me, a sinner. You remember? It is 'The Prayer.' Remember to pray 'The Prayer' always, and everything will be OK. It is the antidote for everything."

"What will be OK, Father?"

"Everything will be OK Christian, everything. We are only passing through this fallen world. This is not our home. We are sinners, Christian. We are screwed without the Lord."

"Screwed?"

"Forgive me but, yes." Demetrius drinks his tea and they watch the hummingbirds fight over the feeder.

"Aren't the hummingbirds beautiful, Christian?"

"Yes, Father Demetrius, they are beautiful, but they are always fighting."

"This is not Eden, Christian. We are far from home. Like the old saying, 'The Lord works in mysterious ways.' It is true. Nothing comes to you that is not at least allowed by the Lord. Everything is meant for your benefit. Keep the Lord in your heart and respond with 'The Prayer' to everything that comes and all will be well."

There is a pregnant pause. Father Demetrius looks at Chris with curiosity.

"Father Demetrius, I have a confession to make."

"Yes, Christian, of course. Let me get my epitrachelion." The father says as he balls up the paper from his bar-b-que, wipes his hands with a napkin and chews his last bite as he reaches into his satchel.

Father Demetrius pulls out the epitrachelion—a long ornate scarf—and a crucifix. He places the scarf around his neck as they both stand. He kisses the scarf and crosses himself three times with the crucifix. Then he holds the crucifix up and looks expectantly at Christian.

Chris hesitates, biting his lip then just blurts it out, "I masturbated 27 times this week."

The father shrugs his shoulders. "Christian, you are a young man. When these evil thoughts come, just say 'The Prayer.' You will make it through these times OK that way."

Chris was obviously relieved at Father Demetrius' response.

"What else?" The Father asks.

"I fantasize about killing Radko. I would never really do it, though."

The Father waited for him to continue.

"...with a golf club. While he is sleeping, a driver, one of those old wooden ones with the metal face on it."

Chris is looking at the floor, shaking his head and wringing his hands, concerned about his sanity.

"I have met Radko. These thoughts are understandable," Father Demetrius says. "We all have bad thoughts, Christian. This is why we confess, to give our burdens to the Lord, so we can be healed."

"Is there anything else, Christian?" The Father cautiously asks.

"Yes... I took part in a pagan ceremony... a peyote ceremony."

"What!" The Father says as a look of horror crosses his face.

"I saw Jesus, Father!" Chris adds with a hopeful smile.

"That was a demon!"

"But Father..."

"It was a demon," the Father says with finality, before adding, "Jesus does not go to a peyote ceremony! This is paganism at its worst. You must stop such behavior before it is too late."

Chris does not know what to think and is saddened by the Father's response. Something has shifted in Chris since his encounter with Jesus during the peyote ceremony. He no longer feels the need for the Father's approval. He feels solid in the Lord.

"Do you have anything else to confess, Christian?"

"No," he lies. He thinks of having sex with Zoie.

"Remember, 'The Prayer' is the antidote for all things, Chris. Use it!"

"OK, Father I will."

The Father closes his eyes and whispers some prayers. He then places the epitrachelion on the top of Chris' head with his palm on it. Chris looks at the floor and says The Lord's Prayer. The Father follows with a quick whispered prayer, makes the sign of the cross on Chris' head and says, "You are forgiven Christian," as he removes the sacred epitrachelion.

"Thank you, Father," Chris says, feeling much lighter. He is even sharper and clearer than before his confession.

"Kiss the cross Christian." Father Demetrius says as he holds it out for Chris to reverence.

"Oh yeah, sorry Father," Chris says, embarrassed at having forgotten the drill. He leans in and kisses the crucifix right on Jesus' crown of thorns.

11

MORTUARY FRONT STREET—SAT.—6:00 PM

CHRIS IS AT THE CURB, peering into the shadows of the mailbox, when he feels the breeze of a sheriff's car streaming past him. It parks at the curb just feet away. He has known a deputy, named Fred, since they were kids. They went to school together. He waits nonchalantly, letters in hand, to see if it is his friend who is in the car.

The car door creaks open and really big man gets out, expanding into the world as he does.

"Hey Buddy!" Fred says stretching the words as he puts on his cowboy hat...

As with many guys of German descent, he is big and rosy-cheeked. His family has been ranching in the area for generations. It is easy to picture him against the blue sky and puffy clouds, with a calf under each arm.

Chris feels a smile stretch across his face as he walks over. Fred grabs Chris by both shoulders and shakes him like a rag doll. "Chris, you look good, man. What is up? Vitamins?"

He lets him loose. "Want to go have a beer?" Fred jokes as he jerks his thumb over his shoulder toward a bar they both know too well.

"I'll have to pass this time." Chris says with a laugh.

When he looks down, he sees the clouds and a hint of blue sky in Fred's mirror-polished shoes.

"I quit drinking again," Chris admits.

"You did?" Fred brightens and stands back, looking skeptical. "Going to meetings?"

"Yeah."

"Got a sponsor?"

"Yeah."

"Who?"

"Henri Purdee."

"Really?"

"Yeah." Chris admits proudly.

"Henri Purdee, huh? He was a bank robber. Everybody knows it."

"I know. I love the guy. He's really been there."

"I'd say and got away with it too!" Fred adds with an admiring tone. "He's helped a lot of people since then. I mean when he got clean and turned his life around. Now he's a Christian I hear."

"Yeah, a minister. That's him nowadays." Chris assures him.

"Go figure, huh? They say when he got back from the war, he shot the hell out of some bank down in the Bahamas with an old style Thompson machine gun. Never did pin it on him, though. Crazy! I wish I had that old Thompson machine gun." Fred looked dreamily into the sky before changing the subject.

"I heard you were spending time with that singer girl, Zoie. Is that true?"

"Not much."

"Be careful Chris. She is as hot as they come and..."

"She just came here for us to take care of her fiancé." Chris interjects. "He died. The morgue is supposed to bring his body here today."

"Chris..."

"I'm just doing my job." Chris pleads in frustration.

"Yeah, I know, but be careful, Chris. Zoie has a history of being S.M.I."

"S.M.I.?"

"Seriously Mentally Ill." The sheriff says gravely. "She's been confined to the state hospital more than once. The whole family is, uh?...nuts. Her father was a rich banker who got on the pipe, a crack addict. He killed himself a few years back. Shot himself in his office while she was out front meeting with clients, covering for him. She lost it after that. Then came terrible living habits and an endless string of men." Fred continues with the grim truth. "She had a ton of money. Spent most of it and gave some away to her dope addict friends. The rest was stolen just recently. She has an off the chart IQ. You are in hot water, man and don't even know it. Be careful!"

"OK...OK." Chris says in surrender.

"She has been with this guy Warren for a couple of months. He's a Yankee!" Fred says, and spits on the ground before continuing. "Spent a few years in prison up there for stealing. Record says he's a safecracker and a really rotten piece of work. I hate to say it...but this is a real boon for our community, him dying like he did."

"I got him on order. We are making arrangements."

"OK well, I guess it's just business then between you and Zoie?"

"Yeah, it's just business. I know crazy when I see crazy."

"Well, I am glad to hear that, Chris. But you know what they say about crazy pussy?"

"Yeah, I know. It's the best pussy," Chris says with a forced laugh, hiding his true feelings.

"We think Warren had a partner. We're trying to find him now."

"Well, I hope you find him soon."

"The poor girl has not got a dime left and doesn't even know it yet," Fred says slowly, shaking his head. "She doesn't have enough money to pay you for the funeral, Chris."

Chis is quiet, not sure what to say or believe, when a call comes in over the radio. Fred tilts an ear and listens for just a second. Then he starts toward his car.

"Sorry Chris gotta go. Remember what I said." He says over his shoulder.

"OK, I will. Nice to see ya, man." Chris shouts.

As Fred leaps into his car and speeds away, the lights come on and the siren screams.

12

MORTUARY RECEPTION ROOM—SUN.—3:33 AM

CHRIS IS ON THE COUCH, in the reception room, finishing the 'Big & Meaty' pizza that he had phoned over from Luigi's. He thought Zoie might want some when she showed up, but he hasn't heard anything from her. He checks the time. It is 3:33 am on Sunday morning. Their appointment was for 6 pm on Saturday. She is now nine hours and thirty-three minutes late.

He takes a deep breath and surveys the damage they did together. The place is a wreck. The couch that he is sitting on—the antique couch with the hand carved wooden legs—the legs are broken. He's replaced them with a stack of moldy red bricks from the garden. The tall gold pleated drapes that were his mother's pride, are heaped on the floor where they fell.

His mother and Radko will be home in a couple of days. There is no way he can get all this cleaned up before they return. His life is like a sinking ship. Fountains of fear and worry erupt through the cracks in the walls of his mind. He needs to run and repair the damage later. They will forgive him eventually, but what about Zoie?

Did he really see Jesus, or was it a hallucination? Chris is torn between two worlds.

Panic envelopes him. He grabs a piece of pizza and wanders the room like a cow chewing its cud at the slaughterhouse door. His mind and emotions are swinging like a storm ravaged pendulum.

"I saw him, damn it," he shouts out loud, looking around for the presence of doubt that is tormenting him. "I know I did. It was real and he loves me." Chris says, shaking his fist at the invisible demon that is moving around the room. It shrinks back, but does not leave.

The struggle for his sanity is too much. Chris feels like he is spinning into nothingness—caught in the breakers of a North Atlantic storm—battered on the levee of rubble that once was his life.

'Maybe I should go look for her?' He says to himself, awash in his own despair. Chris is somewhere between a profound spiritual revelation and pure animal lust. He is afraid that he cannot control himself when he is alone with her again. Images flash through his mind of her naked body. He can smell her scent and glances around, expecting to see her, but she is not there.

One moment he is captured in her, the next he is weeping at the foot of the cross. His soul feels like it is cleaving off and falling into the black abyss. After his encounter with the Lord, Chris is teetering at the edge of Hell.

"Oh God, help me!" Chris prays aloud from the depths of his soul. His prayer is answered by a barrage of thoughts and images. They were not married, but what difference should that make? Why was it wrong? He loves her! What about marriage?

What does marriage have to do with anything? He just wants to have sex with her again. What comes after that is what comes, that's all. What the hell? She has not answered any of his calls or texts anyway.

Maybe he has gone mad from the peyote? That might be alright. She is crazy and he loves her, anyway. So crazy is OK, but Chris has zero tolerance for tardiness!

"Fuck you," he shouts out loud at Zoie wherever she might be, but he instantly regrets it. His heart aches for her. He just wants to hold her and know she is alright.

"Go look out the window," the calm familiar voice says out loud, from right in the middle of the room.

Chris goes to the long tall window next to the door. He jerks aside the lace curtain and peeps out with one eye. His iris dilates. Zoie and a stranger are coming up the steps leading to the front door. As usual, Zoie is in a micro-skirt with heels.

He checks the stranger out as they come closer. 'What a sleaze-ball,' he says to himself.

The man is in a cheap poorly fit suit with multiple rings on his fingers. A flower—just like Radko's—is in his lapel.

'Weird,' thinks to himself. 'There must be a factory somewhere? Looks Italian? Pretty tough looking, too. I've got to do something.' Chris can see from the man's animated gestures—that he desperately wants something from Zoie—but he cannot hear what they are saying.

Outside...

"Where'd Warren put the envelope, the little yellow envelope with an 'IBAN' number in it? He told me it was in a safe place, but wouldn't talk about it on the phone. He was supposed to give me my copy of it yesterday."

The doorbell's soft chimes massage the room. Chris hesitates. This guy scares him, but he would walk into a tiger's cage just to stand next to Zoie. He unhooks the stupid little safety chain, twists the sticky deadbolt free and swings the door open.

"What'd you say was in it again?" Zoie is asking the guy.

"A little yellow envelope," the man says to Zoie. He's oblivious to Chris' presence.

"Oh, Chris, this is Maxey. We just met," Zoie says blithely as she breezes past Chris and into the room. She pads straight across the carpet and drops cross legged onto the lemon-yellow couch that she and Chris destroyed Friday morning. "I just love this couch!" Zoie exclaims as she runs her hands over the fabric.

"How ya doing?" Maxey asks extending his hand. Chris reaches to accept his handshake. Maxey jerks his hand back and makes like he is combing his hair as he follows Zoie in.

'What a loser.' Chris thinks to himself.

Maxey is smacking his gum and looking around the room like he might buy the place. "I hear people are just dying to get in here, yeah," he says, laughing his joke off with a wave of his hand.

Again Maxey offers his hand and Chris dares to accept his handshake. It feels like a dead fish. Chris wipes his palm on his pants as Maxey continues into the center of the room. He is turning slowly—holding his hands out—like a Sufi dancer. "Nice digs, man," he says.

Zoie reaches into her oversized handbag and pulls out a big red Bible. She opens it on her lap. "Guess what I just read, you two? Oh, I knew you'd get along." She says with a squirm of delight, snapping her fingers into the air in affirmation.

"What did ya read, Shuga?" Maxey asks her as he winks at Chris and smacks his gum.

"We've just got to command him to get out of the box. Command him! We don't take no for an answer, no we don't." Zoie is positively euphoric. "It is going to be so wonderful to have Warren back in my arms."

"What?" Chris hears himself croak. 'What is she talking about?' He wonders and concludes, 'I guess my woman is not here yet.'

He starts toward the bar. A vivid image of Henri Purdee beating the shit out of him stops him dead in his tracks. As he pauses, it becomes crystal clear. He turns to her. "What do you really mean, Zoie?" He asks her with the caring tone of an expensive psychiatrist.

"I want you to resurrect Warren for me," she says it, like she is asking him to bring in the groceries.

"Resurrect? What? What do you mean, resurrect?" Chris asks—looking a little lost—like a man who just took a hard blow to the head.

"You are a Christian. It says right here in the Bible. You can do it. I mean—bring him back from the dead."

Chris is now wondering if he has lost his mind and is searching for an answer. 'Maybe this is not happening at all? Maybe this is just a nightmare?'

Chris shakes his head, "It can't... I... I," he feels dizzy and looks for a chair to sit in.

"It says right here, Jesus said, 'You will do greater things than I.'"

"What are you, nuts? But that was Jesus. I...I'm not Jesus." Chris is immediately regretful that he asked if she was nuts. He loves her.

"Watch how you speak to the lady here." Maxey insists, smacking his gum and feigning civility.

"Chris..." Zoie says.

Maxey steps over to Chris and with his back to Zoie, he speaks to Chris in a close whisper. "Just humor her, OK? We takes the body out. Give this resurrection business a try and when it doesn't work, we bring it back."

"Take the body out? Take it where, what, wait, why?!"

"She wants to go to his favorite spot. Some tree somewhere on a hill, where they used to get it on. I don't know. That's where we're going to do it."

"We can't do this. There are laws about how bodies must be handled. There are severe penalties. I can't do this. It would put us out of business and I'd go to jail."

Maxey pulls back his sport coat just enough to reveal a pistol in a leather shoulder holster. He smiles at Chris with the black eyes and gleaming teeth of an approaching shark.

"I know you can do this, Chris...please." Zoie pleads, oblivious to Maxey's veiled threat.

"Why don't you just do it for her?" Maxey asks sympathetically.

Zoie continues, "I am not a believer. You are Chris. You're all I have."

"Yeah, you're all she has," Maxey says as he traces his cheek—with an index finger—as if tracing the tracks of his tears. "Boo-Hoo," he says, mocking Zoie, "Boo-Hoo." Chris can see Zoie in soft focus behind Maxey, looking at them.

For a moment, Chris feels like he is falling into an elevator shaft. He's trapped in his own family's house, with two desperate psychotics. They will destroy everything if he lets them.

13

MORTUARY BASEMENT—SUN.—4:10 AM

THE COFFIN IS ROCKING gently on the warped metal dolly, as Chris pushes it around the corner and continues down the hall. They are going to the loading dock. White tags hang from the brass handles. They declare 'Human Remains' in big red letters.

"We should just take it to UPS, huh?" Maxey says laughing, rapping his knuckles on the coffin's lid as he smacks his gum.

Chris glances back at Zoie. She is behind them and in a bubbly mood. She's reading aloud from the Bible, as if it were a guidebook for the resurrection of the dead and other daily miracles.

She reads out loud, *"When Jesus was in Capernaum, Jairus, a leader in the synagogue, begged him to heal his 12-year-old daughter because she was dying... On the way, a messenger said not to bother because the girl had died, but Jesus said to Jairus, 'Don't be afraid; only believe, and your daughter will be healed.'"*

Just as Zoie finishes, they are passing a well lit storage room. "Hey hold up," she says and goes into the room. She is gathering candles, holders and a lighter into an open cardboard box.

Maxey leans over the coffin to Chris. "This bitch is really crazy. You know what they say about crazy pussy?" Chris ignores him.

While she is out of earshot, Maxey continues. "Maybe you can help us both out here?" Chris just looks at him and the pistol's bulge in his sport coat.

"The stiff in the box was a partner of mine. We had a deal and the son of a bitch goes 'off the clock' before I get my cut."

"OK." Chris is at a loss for what else to say.

"I want my cut. She won't talk to me, but she'll talk to you. You get me the bank numbers...and I'll disappear like Casper the Ghost," he says with a smile and a magical wave of his hands. Then he turns ice cold. "I'll waste her, boy. I'll hurt her, then I'll waste her." Maxey sees Zoie returning and lowers his voice.

"I am counting on you," he says, smacking his gum vigorously.

"What are you going to do with all those candles, Shuga?" Maxey asks her.

"You'll see," she says excitedly, adding, "It's going to be so beautiful."

When they get to the loading dock, Chris opens the back of the hearse. He slips the coffin right off the gurney into the hearse and secures it inside.

Zoie is looking confused. Chris takes the box of candles from her and puts them in the side door. Her mood has dropped. She looks like she is trying to remember something.

Chris opens the driver's door and waits for her to come around. Maxey comes over and inserts himself between them.

"I'm driving," he says then lowering his voice, "Get that crazy bitch in here."

Zoie is frozen, looking through the glass on the side of the hearse.

"Zoie," Chris says.

"I can't believe he is in there. In that box," she says.

Chris goes and guides her to the passenger side door. With a little coaxing, she gets in.

"I forgot to take my pills. I mean, I went to get my refills last night. All my cards were declined. I don't understand. So I'm out of pills. I'm not feeling like myself. I'm sorry," she weeps.

"It's OK," Chris lies, wondering if they will survive the trip at all.

Zoie snuggles as close to Chris as she can. Maxey turns the key. The warm rumble from the engine brings a sense of security to all of them. The cabin is illuminated by the green instrument lights. Zoie is studying Chris' features. "Sometimes I wish I had met you first," she says simply.

Chris looks into her liquid eyes, then glances past her to Maxey, who mouths clearly, 'Get the number.'

14

MORTUARY GARAGE—SUN.—5:00 AM

"OK. GIMME THE DIRECTIONS." Maxey says like a poker player calling to see the cards.

Zoie takes out her phone, brings up the navigation, then hangs it on the dash by the magnetic holder. Chris leans to look at the map. "Just 1.5 hours. We should get there just about sunrise." Chris says.

Maxey squints at the phone, rubs his chin, "That looks pretty simple, just follow the arrow, huh?" Chris and Zoie glance at each other in disbelief. Maxey gives it a little gas and they move down the drive toward the street.

When the open window reaches him, the cat on the wall howls into Maxey's ear. "What the fuck!" Maxey screams, gripping the wheel in sheer terror. When he realizes it was just an old alley cat, he is embarrassed. He takes a long breath and quickly regains his usual grim composure.

'Somehow I need to get rid of that gun.' Chris thinks to himself.

"No!" Chris is startled by the same voice that spoke to him in the living room.

Zoie traces Chris' earlobe with her finger. "If I had not met Warren first, it would be you," she says wistfully, biting her lips and batting her eyes.

'She's crazy.' Chris reminds himself. He tries not to want her as she snuggles in even closer. Her scent and the sound of her breathing makes him dizzy.

When they come to the first stoplight—he considers jumping out of the car to run for help—but that would leave Zoie alone with a psychopathic killer. 'Maybe I could get to the police and they could stop this,' he tries to rationalize but realizes that is not likely to work out.

'Please God, help us,' he prays silently as he looks at Zoie and the madman behind the wheel. Trying to calm himself, he asks her, "You ever think of moving to Nashville, Zoie?"

"Oh yeah. All the time."

"I want to go to Austin, to The Comedy Mothership."

"You should, Chris. You should. When I get Warren back, we are going to move to Nashville."

"Yeah right." Maxey says, rolling his eyes and flicking his cigarette butt out the window.

They roll into a fog bank. Maxey slows down to a very low speed.

Zoie realizes something. "I think we need to ask God for forgiveness for our sins to be pure enough to resurrect Warren."

Chris tries to be helpful, "Zoie, it seems to me..."

"What's that say?" Maxey says, pointing at a big green highway sign ahead.

"Exit to Liberty Hill." Chris says, surprised that Maxey is illiterate.

"Zoie," Chris says to her. "Maxey is looking for some bank numbers that Warren had for him. Do you know where they are?"

She looks at Chris and just smiles dreamily. "Oh yeah, of course I do. They say it is on the hill. That's right. I remember now."

"They?" Chris asks.

"Shut up, see what she says." Maxey insists.

Zoie continues, recollecting. "He buried the number—the little yellow envelope—on our hill in a peanut butter jar."

"Yeah!" He exclaims, "Yeah!" Maxey is pounding on the steering wheel.

"Do you remember exactly where, Zoie?" Maxie asks her.

"Yes, of course, near the tree. You'll see when we get there. I want Maxey to get what is coming to him," she says, turning to Chris and putting a hand on his knee. "I have been praying for it and the angels helped me to remember."

"Angels?" Maxey asks...

"Do you know how many times that raising the dead is mentioned in the Bible?" Zoie asks with a tone of amazement...

She shifts her weight onto Chris' shoulder and is quickly asleep with the Bible open on her lap.

Chris looks at their reflection in the window. In the midst of all this chaos, he feels lucky. They ride in silence for a long time. The fog is not letting up. What should have been a 90-minute trip is taking a lot longer.

Later...

The Sun is slowly breaking through in patches, bringing warm highlights to the rain-soaked fields. The navigation says they are near the destination. They roll slowly, looking for landmarks.

"It's a big hill," she says, "with a beautiful tree on top."

"It says we're there. It says we're there," Maxey repeats impatiently before adding, "You better be right."

Tension rings through Chris' tired body. He repeats 'The Prayer' silently to himself.

"There it is!" Zoie says, pointing up a hill with a lone tree on top. She is hopping in her seat from excitement. Zoie looks back through the window at the coffin. "It won't be long now, Honey. It won't be long and we'll be together again."

15

THE HILL—SUN.—7:15 AM

"WELL, LET ME JUST GET my little yellow envelope and...," Maxey is grumbling when something catches their attention. There are shadows moving in the remaining fog down the road.

"What the fuck?" Maxey asks out loud.

"They're here." Zoie says quietly.

About a dozen people walk out of the fog bank on the wet two-lane country road. "Migrants," Chris says aloud, "out of Mexico." The remnants of their past are stuffed into day packs and plastic shopping bags.

"Let me out...let me out!" Zoie shouts. She starts to climb over Chris. He gets out to set her free.

The migrants come to a dead stop and look in their direction.

"Shit!" Maxey says as he slaps the steering wheel with his palm.

Zoie heads right toward the migrants while Maxey and Chris meet in front of the car. "What the fuck?" Maxey says sarcastically with a wave of his hand. "Where'd all these beaners come from?"

'There's safety in numbers,' Chris thinks to himself. 'This just might be our rescue party.'

There are ten or twelve men and women with one child, a boy, about six years old. He is clearly mentally disabled. Zoie crosses the wet road and speaks to them in Spanish, while Maxey and Chris wait by the hearse.

"Hey get away from me, you fucking retard." The boy was reaching into Maxey's pocket.

"What the fuck, man?" Chris asks. "That kid didn't do anything to you."

"These people are like cockroaches," Maxey says. "You don't see them and then they are on ya."

The boy runs into the grassy field to play among the dandelions and butterflies.

"Wow." Chris says at Maxey.

"That shit's contagious. I don't care what they say." Maxey says, in defense of himself.

Zoie is across the street asking the migrants to help her carry the coffin up the hill. They all step forward to follow her.

"Maxey! We cannot have any negative energy here now." Zoie says as she and the migrants pass by.

Maxey catches up to Zoie and walks alongside her. "Let's just get this shit over with. I want that envelope, Zoie," he says in a snarling whisper, "or you and lover boy here won't be leaving this hill."

The men step in and create a barrier between Maxey and Zoie. They glare at Maxey with a strange authority.

Maxey stops in his tracks. It is clear he will have to wait.

"I am so sorry for what that man said to your boy," Chris says to a woman as they walk behind Zoie.

"He is not mine. He travels alone, like most of us. His name is Miguel."

When they get to the hearse, Zoie opens the side door and hands the candles out to the women. Chris opens the rear door, then helps the men get the coffin out and onto their shoulders.

Zoie takes off her heels and tosses them into the hearse. She looks around at the men and women. All nod in silent agreement and the pallbearers start across the road toward the hill. The peasant women fall behind—in their role as mourners—comforting Zoie, who is now weeping. They hold her as if she were one of their own. With the women singing in Spanish, the ragged but devoted procession heads up the hill. The coffin is bobbing on the shoulders of six strong young men.

The hillside is grassy and wet. There are a couple of slips and near falls, but the Sun warms them and gives them strength. When they get to the top, most of the fog has burned off. The Sun is radiating golden streamers under the vast blue dome.

In the speckled light, under the canopy of the great tree, the men gently place the coffin on the ground. Maxey pants as he slumps against the tree's enormous trunk. He pulls a handkerchief out of his sweat-soaked shirt pocket and mops his brow with it.

16

THE HILLTOP—SUN.—8:02 AM

ZOIE LOOKS AROUND AND thanks everyone for their help. They form a circle around her and the coffin as she retrieves the Bible from her bag.

Chris is surprised at how calm he feels. He continues to repeat 'The Prayer' under his breath and knows deeply that all is good and all is in God's hands.

Zoie opens the Bible, takes a breath and looks around kindly at all the people in the circle. She begins to read: *"Luke 7:11—Soon afterwards, Jesus went to a city called Nain; and His disciples were going along with Him, accompanied by a large crowd. Now as He approached the gate of the city, a dead man was being carried out, the only son of his mother, and she was a widow; and a sizable crowd from the city was with her. When the Lord saw her, He felt compassion for her, and said to her, do not weep and He came up and touched the coffin; and the bearers came to a halt. And He said, Young man, I say to you, arise! The dead man sat up and began to speak. And Jesus gave him back to his mother. Fear gripped them all, and they began glorifying God, saying, A great prophet has arisen among us! And God has visited His people! This report concerning Him went out all over Judea and in all the surrounding district."*

When she closes the Bible, there is a tremendous crack of thunder and a lightning bolt strikes in their midst.

When they come to their senses, the migrants are gone. Scattered candles are smoldering on the ground where they had been.

Maxey is crawling around frantically. "Where's my gun? Where'd they go?" He repeats, "Where's my gun? Where'd they go?"

"Back to Heaven," Chris says in disappointment. "You never know when you are in the company of angels," he says, shaking his head as they get up.

"Where's my gun?" Maxey repeats.

"Is that it?" Chris says, pointing to a twisted piece of metal smoldering on the ground.

A child's laughter pierces the scene. All three of them look. Little Miguel has both palms on the coffin lid and is looking at them with an all-knowing smile.

"Oh, no you don't." Chris says.

"Yes...please do it," Zoie says, affirming her prayer.

Miguel disappears and the coffin lid blows off, twisting and flipping into the air. It lands far away in a distant field.

Zoie, Chris and Maxey are saucer eyed and slack jawed. Warren's corpse sits up like a jack-in-the-box on Halloween. His face is lumpy, green, black and yellow. There is a gaping laceration across his neck and he is covered in brown dried blood.

They all step back three paces in unison. Warren shakes himself as if he is waking up from a deep and restful sleep. He checks his tie, then steps out of the coffin onto the ground.

"Holy shit!" Maxey says.

Chris looks at Zoie and says simply, "I don't think Jesus did it this way."

"Ugh!" She is revolted by Warren's appearance.

Warren looks around, confused, as if his elevator has stopped at the wrong floor.

"He looks like the walking dead." Zoie says.

"He is." Chris agrees.

"Oh, my God." Zoie says.

"What the fuck?" Warren says hoarsely, holding his throat, "How did I get here?"

"We resurrected you or actually Zoie did," Chris says, pointing to her.

"What? You resurrected me!"

"Well, technically God did. We just followed the directions." Zoie says with a shrug of her shoulders and a hopeful smile.

"I was in Heaven! You brought me back to this shit hole?"

"How did you ever get into Heaven?" Chris wonders out loud.

"Well?" Warren responds thoughtfully, "I was laying there face down in the glass and I muttered a prayer to Jesus. Next thing I knew, I was in Heaven. It was amazing and now I'm back here?" He scans the area with disbelief. "What the fuck?!"

"You shouldn't swear Warren. It's a sin," Zoie reminds him before adding, "I'm leaving you for Chris here," she says, pointing to Chris.

"Nice to meet ya," Chris mutters with a slight wave, at a loss for words.

"You brought me back to this, this—Hell—just to break up with me?"

"I just don't love you anymore, Warren."

"Where's my money, you son of a bitch?!" Maxey said with a rabid snarl, "Where's the bank account numbers?"

Warren looks at Maxey with deep loathing and searches his pockets. He pulls the little yellow envelope out of his sport coat, looks at it for a moment, then holds it out to Maxey.

"Here they are," Warren says. Maxey balks at the invitation, but Warren continues, "What are you afraid of? You're just a scaredy boy, huh? Here it is. The account number is in this envelope. It will make you millions, but you are afraid. Oh, Boo-Hoo." Warren says, tracing the tracks of the invisible tears on his cheek.

"Fuck!" Maxey shouts. He steps forward—reaches out and takes the envelope. Warren grabs him by the neck with both hands and throttles him. Chris looks around and picks up a softball sized stone off the ground. He runs over and hits Warren on the head with it.

When Warren falls, Maxey runs off down the hill. He slips and falls, but gets back up. Then he is struck by a lightning bolt out of the clear blue sky. There is nothing left but a human shaped, black cloud of cinders, falling to the ground.

Warren gets up and glares at Zoie. "You God damned bitch," he shouts and he starts toward her.

Chris is turning to defend her when a voice declares, "That is all I needed."

The earth breaks open next to Warren and the Devil himself pops up from Hell and grabs Warren by the arm.

"It's the Devil," Chris says in horror.

"Oh, thank God." Zoie says with a sigh of relief. "My God they stink," she adds, holding her stomach and covering her mouth like she will puke.

Chris pulls out his big crucifix and holds it up between them and the Devil. The Devil recoils at the sight of it. "Lord Jesus Christ, have mercy on us," Chris prays as he covers his mouth and nose with his free hand.

The Devil is naked with gleaming red salamander skin, a tail, horns and withered little wings. He stands on goat's legs and cloven hooves. His claws are wrapped around Warren's arm like a vise. His black spherical, shrimp like eyes inspect his latest catch as he says, "So here's another one that almost got away. These last-minute confessions rarely work out." The Devil looks at Chris and Zoie with a satisfied smile, then returns his attention to Warren, who is saucer eyed and quaking with fear. "You have to really believe, Warren. Now you see, don't you? True believers act like true believers. We were watching you the whole time. So obvious. If only you had really repented and been forgiven, but now's too late!" The Devil's laugh echoes off the blue dome of the sky.

Then he looks at Chris and Zoie and speaks to them slowly, as if they were kindergarteners. "Everybody knows you must repent and forgive to be forgiven. You have to be really, really sorry and never ever want to do it again. Everybody knows that but Warren and a few hundred million others. You see, Warren wasn't sorry. He was just scared and scared isn't good enough."

The Devil pauses and smiles broadly before continuing. "I can't be all that bad. I saved your life. He would have killed you. He's such a bad boy, one of my favorites," he says with the wink of an eye. "There are so many bad ones here. I just love Texas."

"I saw the whole thing from right over there," he admits as he reaches his long arm out and points toward an empty treeless field.

"Nearly had you too," he says to Chris, "but you are saying His name. One day you will stop saying His name, then you will be mine."

The Devil looks Zoie up and down for a moment. Then he speaks like the uncouth dice roller that he really is. "I just love that tiny skirt, you little temptress, you and all those lovers." He adds with a wag of his long bony finger, "Keep that up and you will be mine forever." Zoie notices he is getting hard.

Repulsed beyond measure, she looks down at herself and she sees her nakedness for the first time. Zoie squirms and tries to hide herself with her hands, but it does not work.

"You have paved your path to my door with broken hearts, missy. Don't bother knocking. Just come on in and come as you are."

She turns into Chris' protective arms. He stuffs the crucifix into his belt, takes off his duster and puts it over Zoie's shoulders. She wraps herself in it, holding her Bible so close to her chest and so tight that it bends. Chris holds his cross back up toward the Devil. With one arm around Zoie, he continues saying 'The Prayer.'

"We will meet again, missy, when you're not reading from that book and he," the Devil points at Chris, "is not saying His name."

"I'll be around," the Devil says with a laugh. A look of horror flashes across Warren's rotten face as the earth opens up and they drop straight into Hell below. The Devil's laughing and Warren's screaming echo into distant silence. Smoke, sparks and flames of fire come out of the hole. Moments later, the hole closes and the ground heals up. Not a trace of the hole is left.

Exhausted, Chris and Zoie fall to their knees and into each other's protective arms. They are struggling to get their breath when a warm and inviting light comes from the side. They look toward the source and cautiously stand to see what it is.

The entire landscape and atmosphere has turned a pure and snowy white. Golden sparks of living light inhabit the ocean of air. They drift in the invisible currents like snowflakes.

The Lord's childlike face shines like the Sun in the sky but with much greater brilliance. He is more beautiful than anything ever seen before. Somehow they are able to gaze into this blinding Heavenly Light and really see for the first time.

"I am so sorry," Zoie says. As the tears course down her cheeks she sobs into her palms. Please forgive me. Light passes through her, rearranging her whole being, mind, body and soul. A new woman now stands there in her place. She is healed, radiant and forgiven. Chris imagines her as the twin sister Zoie never had. She is perfect—sinless and unblemished—more beautiful than ever before.

"Thank you, thank you," Zoie repeats solemnly. With her face awash in tears of surrender, she drops to her knees.

Chris, also radiant, is looking into the face of the Lord and weeping as only a 'Fool for Love' can. Everything is forgiven—everything is understood—everything is Blessed.

At Zoie's feet, the little yellow envelope rests. It is singed around the edges, but it contains all the riches the world has to offer.

About the Author

Jack Webb was born in South Carolina, then raised mostly on U.S. Air Force bases, in Europe and the southwestern U.S. After graduating from college, he became involved in the motion picture industry and eventually became a director of photography. While working in film production, Jack honed his addictions to a fine edge. Now, with many years of sobriety under his belt, he has taken to writing short stories. These stories are based on real-life experiences, tales he has heard told and his own vivid imagination. This is his first novella.

Read more at https://jackwebbwriter.com.